Gawain and the Green Knight

Gawain and the Green Knight

Adventure at Camelot

By Y. R. PONSOR

Illustrated by Darrell Sweet

MACMILLAN PUBLISHING CO., INC.
New York
COLLIER MACMILLAN PUBLISHERS
London

Macmillan Publishing Co., Inc.
866 Third Avenue, New York, N.Y. 10022
Collier Macmillan Canada, Ltd.

Library of Congress Cataloging in Publication Data
Ponsor, Y R
Gawain and the Green Knight.
1. Gawain—Romances. I. Gawain and the Green
Knight.
PR2065.G306P6   821'.1   79-12940
ISBN 0-02-598000-9

First Printing 1979

Designed by Jack Meserole

Printed in the United States of America

This book is dedicated to the First
Maker and to all those in between

CONTENTS

FOREWORD

"Gawain and the Green Knight," of which this book is a prose adaptation, is a poem written about 1400 by an unknown author. The period is Chaucerian, but the Lancashire dialect is unfamiliar even to those who can read Chaucer easily. It retains more of the elements of Old English than are found in Chaucer: the "thorn" and the "yoke"; the strong alliterative line; the complex rhyme scheme that sets off the bob - and - wheel closing each stanza. I have attempted to keep the flavor of the poem by the rhythm of language, most apparent when read aloud, and by the occasional specific, if strange, word. Why translate? Why adapt? I have chosen to give up the form for the spirit in order to make the story more accessible to the general reader.

Gawain still speaks to us today. There is nothing archaic or anachronistic about the message. He holds up a mirror—a polished shield, perhaps—in which we may catch a glimpse of a finer self. Gawain lives, as we do, in a particular time and place. He is, as we are, a product of his culture. He has been insulated by his own myth, his humanity buried under the gear of knighthood, however grand and protective it may be. His culture has made him a symbol, a standard against which all men measure themselves. But man as symbol is no more human than man as machine, and his problem is a modern problem: how to live in this world as a human being. Although he "falls," it is a fortunate fall indeed, for it is into something greater. He is human; that is the necessary lesson of his quest and testing. As a human being, Gawain knows his own nature, and the court heals his scars with love and sharing.

This, I think, is the lesson that must be repeated time and time again. We live in a world that seems to eliminate our humanness by shoving us into molds and costumes. We have learned to apologize for being human. We lose, then, the sense of self that requires honor and love and responsibility and forgiveness. It is as true today as it was in 1400: To be human is painful, dangerous, and sometimes full of dread. It is also grand, exciting, and full of wonder. It is what we are. If we are ever to know our humanity, we must do our best to reach it.

Gawain and the Green Knight

PROLOGUE

After the fall of Troy, the long siege and assault having ended, Aeneas, the Trojan prince, left the burning city under cover of confusion and darkness. He led his young son by the hand and carried his old father on his back, and often as he fled he looked back at the flames flaring to the sky, to the smoke rising from that suffering city conquered by treachery as much as by force of arms. The fabled towers of Ilium were soon to be burnt to brands and ashes, its noble inhabitants delivered to death or scattered into slavery, and all its glory would fade into a remembered vision in the blind eyes of old Homer.

But Aeneas, with the help of the gods—his mother was Venus, after all!—and after many adventures, came at last to Alba Longa, and founded his kingdom. With the passage of time his royal descendants subdued all of the area, even to the Western Isles; and then Brutus crossed the French flood and founded his kingdom upon the broad shores and fair fields of Britain. Bold was that breed of men! And since that day have come war and woe, blessing and blunder, turn by turn, and many a marvel besides.

Of all Britain's kings, the most worthy of fame was Arthur. Many tales have been told of this man, as all men know, and I intend to show you a true adventure of those days, the fine first age of these men, these fairest folk under heaven's blessing. Some may call this a marvel, a miracle even, and certainly it is an exceeding strange happening. So if you will listen for a while, I will tell it as I have heard it told.

Chapter 1

WINTER lay upon the land. Cold held forest and field in its grim clutch, and in the night sky the stars glittered like gems. The wolf slid from shadow to shadow, stalking hapless prey, falling upon the unwary with death in his fangs. Deep in caverns the great trolls and other monsters mumbled in uneasy sleep, seeking warmth. Over moor and fen the mists rose and fell, and strange sounds troubled the chill silence.

But on the hill lights gleamed in the castle. In the court of Camelot were gathered all the brothers-in-arms of the Table Round and their fair highborn ladies to celebrate the Christmas season. A full fifteen days it was then, a time of merriment and mirth and rich revel. Laughter rang loud through the halls, and all the music and delight that the mind of man might devise. With merrymaking and glee the company welcomed the New Year, exchanging gifts and calling out glad Noel.

On this New Year's day, fresh and crisp-cold, twice the usual number of celebrants crowded the great hall; and the most noble, the fairest, and most famous was Arthur himself, the most honorable man who ever ruled a court or led an army into battle. This king was a man of the greatest good will and generosity of soul, and it would be difficult to imagine a bolder company than that one gathered in the castle on the hill.

Among the group on the high dais facing the great hall lined with tables of noble knights was Guenevere, Arthur's wife, the comeliest maid, the gracious lady of the gleaming gray eyes. Her silken garments sparkled with rich jewels and her golden hair shone as softly as her eyes. With her sat the young Gawain, with Agravaine the Stronghand on the other side; both were the king's nephews and worthy knights who had proved their prowess many times in test and trial. At the head of the table sat the chief of all bishops in Cornwall, the saintly Bedwin, and with him, Urien's son Iwain.

But Arthur, full of his own happiness and childlike in his joy, would not sit until all were served. For most of all he loved life, its joys and its adventures, and his eager brain and young blood would not allow him to lie abed or sit around lazily. And besides, he had taken upon himself a vow that on this special day of all days, he would not eat until a rare tale of ancestors and arms and high adventure were told, or some grand marvel might be devised, or a challenge of knights to join in jeopardy, jousting life for life as fortune might favor. So he stood before the high table, speaking of trifles and laughing at the noise and fine festival of his free men as the first course was announced with the crackling of trumpets, with drums and tuneful pipers. In the corner a bard awakened the lute and many a heart lifted with his touch upon the strings. Then came the platters piled high with fine food, venison and other meats, and great bowls of soup, and a plenty of strong beer and fine red wine. And all drank and ate as much as they wanted.

Hardly had the first course been finished when the great hall door crashed open and in rode a terrifying knight. He must have been the hugest man on earth, so broad and thick from neck to waist, so long of leg and strong of arm that I half thought him a giant, except for his fine features of face. Everyone knows that giants are hideous to look upon, besides being fearful in size. At sight of him, all in the hall fell silent, struck dumb by this apparition. For this bold man, from toe to top, in clothes and in countenance, was bright green.

Believe me: all garbed in green, this man, and all his trappings. He wore a tight coat with a heavy mantle adorned with ermine, the same fur lining the hood that had fallen from his head and lay upon his shoulders. Green were the stockings on his legs, and decorated with gold embroidery, and bright golden spurs on his feet, and shoes with upturned toes. His belt was set with gleaming jewels, all emerald green, and indeed they were scattered over all his array and that of his horse, the saddle and bridle and reins, all gaudy in gold and green. The trappings of the horse, the breast-cloth and bits and bridle, even the stirrups in which he stood, all were enameled and gleamed goldenly, and the green gems glittered like the eyes of a cat. The steed itself which he straddled was a great heavy horse, hard to hold; and it was the same green as the man who rode it.

Gloriously was this man outfitted in green, and the hair of his head as green as his horse. It fanned out full and fell to his shoulders, and he had a heavy beard which reached his chest. It gleamed green upon the leather tunic. Such a pair had never before been seen on earth, nor since that time! Everyone said he looked as bright as a flash of lightning, and, indeed, who could withstand his stroke! He wore neither helm nor hauberk—no, no coat of mail did he wear, nor want!—and he carried no weapons, neither spear nor shield to smite or to save. But in his hand he carried a bough of holly, that branch which is greenest when all others are bare; and in his other hand an ax, heavy and horrid, a cruel weapon right out of a nightmare. The head measured at least an arm's length, and was of green steel worked with gold, the bit burnished bright, the broad edge honed to shear as closely as a sharp razor. The steel of the haft which he held in his hand was wrapped with iron wire to its very end, graven with green in delicate design. A thong bound it about and fastened at the head where it was tasseled and braided with bright green.

This knight moved through the great hall's silent crowd right up to the high table, and he feared no danger, greeted no one, but looked straight ahead. Then he reined in his horse and faced the room. He stared boldly at the knights, looking them up and down, and his voice thundered when he spoke.

"Where is the leader of this company? I would like to see

him and to speak in courtesy with him, as the rules of chivalry require."

He waited and looked at them and considered who might among this company be the most renowned.

Everyone stared at him in wonder, marveling as to what his appearance might mean, how such a knight and such a horse might be such a strange color, green as growing grass, and glowing with enamel and gold. Everyone studied him as he sat there on his horse, and they walked cautiously around him with all the wonder in the world as to what he might do. Many strange things had they seen, but never any such as this. Possibly a phantom, or some fey creature, they deemed him to be, for green is a magic color. But all of these brave knights feared to question him and, stunned at his voice, were dumbstruck. A heavy silence filled the royal chamber, and all those who had been chattering sat as if caught in a dream—some, I suppose, out of politeness, some out of uneasiness, and some in fear, but let another man decide which!

Then Arthur, standing before the dais, greeted him, and bowed courteously, for he was never rude, and said,

"Fair knight, welcome to this place. I am Arthur, the chief of this company. Alight and rest, I beg you, and whatsoever your will may be, we shall be glad to learn."

"No, God is my witness that to waste time in idle talk is not my errand," replied the knight. "But your fame, lord, is raised high, and through town and countryside you are regarded as the best and bravest ever to ride in battle gear, the noblest and the finest of the world's kind. You are all known to be valiant in dealing with all sorts of adventures, and your hall is known for courtliness. Many tales of this company have reached my ears, and that is what has brought me hither at this special time.

"You may see by this branch which I bear here that I have come in peace, seeking no trouble; for had I fared forth in a frame of mind to fight, I would have brought helm and hauberk, and shield and bright-shining spear, and other weapons to wield also. But because I seek no strife, I am dressed as you see. But if you are as brave as everyone says, you will gladly grant me the game that I ask as a guest's right."

And Arthur answered, "Gentle knight, if you crave combat, you will not fail to find it here."

"No, I seek no contest, as I have told you, especially since I see on these benches only beardless children! If I were geared up for fighting and mounted on my high steed, there is no man here who could match me." And he looked upon them with scorn. "I seek in this court only a Christmas game, for it is Yule and the New Year, and the time to exchange gifts. If there should be any in this hall who considers himself brave enough in heart, hot enough in blood, or quick enough of wit that he would dare exchange stroke for stroke with me, let him come forth. I will give him as my gift this fine heavy ax—heavy enough it is to do his will!—and I shall take the first blow as bare as here I sit. If any of these fine warriors may be so bold as to accept my challenge, let him step forth and seize this weapon. I quitclaim it forever, and he may keep it as his own, and I shall kneel before him and stand him a stroke. And then you will grant me the right to deal him an equal blow, though I will give him respite of a year and a day. Now let any man who so dares speak quickly."

Chapter II

IF the people had been astonished at first, now they all, high and low throughout the hall, sat as if turned to stone. The knight on his steed twisted in the saddle, his red eyes flashing around the room, his green hair flying with each movement of his head. Then he sat still, staring at them and stroking his beard as the silence lengthened. When no one spoke, he stood in his stirrups and, shaking his fist above his head, he shouted at them.

"What is this? Is this Arthur's court and castle, of which the whole world sings praises? Where now is your pride? Where is your fighting spirit? Where now your fierceness and fame and all your fine words? Now is the reputation and glory of the Round Table overthrown by the mere words of one man, without a single blow being struck, because you are afraid to answer!"

Then the blood shot for shame into Arthur's face, and he turned as angry as a storm-wind, as indeed did all of them. Men muttered and surged forward in anger, half-rising from their places, white with wrath. But Arthur held up his hand and sprang to face the green man.

"Sir, by heaven! Seek no further! As you in your own folly have asked, so shall it be! No man here is afraid of your boasts. Give me your ax, and with God's help, I shall break every bone in your body. I myself accept your challenge and will meet your terms."

The Green Knight laughed aloud and leaped lightly from his horse and landed before Arthur, taller by head and shoulders than any man in the court. The king seized the ax and gripped the handle tightly and waved it about, striking this way and that to test its feel. The knight calmly removed his mantle and then his short coat, no more dismayed by the threatening blows than if some man had brought him a glass of wine.

Then Gawain, who sat by the queen, called out, "I beseech you, uncle, to grant me a kindness. Let this contest be mine. Gentle lord, give me permission to leave this table and stand in your place there. If I may without discourtesy—if my liege lady will not take it amiss—I would presume to counsel you before your royal court." He stood up and spoke clearly. "I think it is not seemly that such a challenge should be raised in this high chamber, much less that you yourself should so valiantly choose to answer it while so many brave warriors remain on these benches. No better men can be found on any field of battle, nor any more skillful in arms. All men know that I am the least brave, and the feeblest of wit, and the least deserving to be of this company. In truth, it is only because I am your nephew that I am worthy at all; I know no bounty but your blood in my body. And since this business is so foolish and trivial, none of it should concern you at all.

"So I ask: Let it come to me, and if I fail in its performance, then the fault is in me and no blame shall fall on this court."

Arthur moved from table to table consulting with his nobles, as is the custom in such cases, and all agreed that the king should retire from the contest and give Gawain the game.

Gawain turned and bowed to the gray-eyed Guenevere and she smiled on him, and he came down from the dais and, kneeling before his king, he received the ax from Arthur's hands. And Arthur smiled affectionately upon him and raised his hand and asked God's blessing, praying that both Gawain's heart and his hand should be strong.

"Be careful, nephew," he said softly, "and set yourself for the stroke. If you direct it properly, I am sure that you will be able to bear the burden of the blow which he will later inflict." And Arthur removed himself and went and leaned against the edge of the dais and watched eagerly.

Gawain walked, ax in hand, to the Green Knight, who had been waiting patiently. He looked upon Gawain and he said, "Now, let us reaffirm our bargain before we go on. But first I would ask you, sir, what is your name?"

"I am Gawain," the young man said. "It is Gawain who gives you this blow, whatever may happen afterwards. One year from now, you may return the favor with whatever weapon you wish, asking leave of no one else."

"By God," shouted the other, "it pleases me greatly that I should receive this blow from your hands. You have rightly repeated the covenant which I made with your king—except that you must seek me, friend, wheresoever you think I may be found, pledging to come alone, and return to me such wages as you deal to me today before this court."

"And where shall I look for you? Where is your home? I know neither your kingdom nor your name, kith nor kin. Tell me your realm and name and I shall certainly find you. That I swear on my honor."

"No," said the green man, "nothing more is necessary now. But I promise that when I have taken your blow, if you strike squarely, then I will tell you how to find me so that you may fulfill our bargain."

Then he laughed.

"If I do not speak, then so much the better for you; you can stay in your own land and light no wayfarer's fires. But enough! Take up your weapon and let us see how you handle an ax!"

"Sir," said Gawain, "I will," and he stroked the edge of the ax.

The Green Knight knelt on the floor and bent his head and gathered his long, thick hair in one hand and drew it over the crown of his head. His bare neck shone whitely. Gawain set himself, left foot forward on the floor. He grasped the ax and lifted it aloft, and he brought it down like a lightning bolt upon the bare neck. The sharp steel sliced through the pale flesh and sundered the bones and sheared it in half, and the steel blade buried itself in the floor with a great ringing crash.

The fair head flew from the shoulders and rolled about near the tables, and some of the knights kicked at it with their feet, a grim, grisly game. Blood burst from the body, red gleaming on green. The knight did not falter or fall, but at once he sprang up on his strong legs and jumped into the crowd and snatched up his head by the hair and lifted it high for all to see. Then, striding to his horse, he caught up the reins, stepped into the stirrups and sat aloft, still holding his head high in one hand.

And they say that he sat in his saddle as though nothing whatever ailed him, headless though he was. He twisted from side to side, turning that hideous, still-bleeding body in the saddle. Those who watched in fear were even more horrified to see that he was about to speak.

He turned the grim face toward the high table, and the head lifted up its eyelids and looked at them. Then it looked at Gawain and the mouth moved and the lips spoke.

"Look to it, Gawain, that you do as you have sworn, and seek faithfully until you find me. All men know me as the knight of the Green Chapel. To the Green Chapel you must come, I charge you, to receive such a blow as you have dealt here to me today. You will find me if you try. If you fail to come, coward shall you be called by the whole world."

With a quick movement he pulled his horse around and fled through the great door, still head-in-hand, and the fire from the hooves of his flint-shod steed flashed through the hall. What native land he would return to, none there knew, any more than they knew from whence he had come. In a moment a roar of astonishment filled the hall, and Arthur and Gawain burst into laughter at the strange event. All agreed that it had been a marvel among men.

Although Arthur, ever the wise king, had a great uneasiness in his heart, he did not let a hint of it be seen, but he spoke to his queen with courtly speech.

"Dearest lady, let not today dismay you. Often such a magic and wondrous event occurs at this season, along with the music of minstrels and the laughter of lovely ladies and brave knights."

And he touched her hand gently and gazed into her eyes. Then he sat back, looked around the room, and cried out, "Now at last I may address myself to my dinner, for I have certainly seen a marvel, I must admit."

He smiled at Gawain with love shining on his fair face and he said, "Hang up your ax, nephew, it has done its work for today." And it was placed on the wall above the high table where all might admire and wonder at the sight and the strange adventure. Then they sat down again at the tables, each to his place, king and knights, and the servants brought double portions of all the best dishes and with all manner of good will they passed the rest of the evening.

But be sure, Sir Gawain, that fear does not cause you to fail in this test, this challenge which you yourself have taken into your own hands!

Chapter III

O this gift was granted to Arthur on the first day of the young year, the bold adventure that he had sought. Indeed a stern duty had been put upon the youth Gawain, one which he must answer. He had been willing enough to accept that wager in the great hall on that festive day among his companions and peers and under the gray gaze of Guenevere. Any man would be glad to show himself courageous and cool when only praise can come for his prowess; but that the end of this endeavor would be grievous, none could doubt. For a man may be merry in his mind when his mouth is full of mead, but time passes, never to return, and the form of its fulfillment seldom unfolds itself. No man knows, upon rising, how the sun will set, whether upon good or ill.

And so in this fashion the Yule passed by and the year-days after it, and each season in turn followed one after another, as the Lord has willed.

After Christmas came the crabbed Lenten season, the great feasts of Christmas giving way to simpler fare. Then the world struggled with winter. Cold held the land in an iron grip and clouds covered the heavens, and all was gray and bleak and bare. Then came shining rain falling in warm showers on field and fold. Soon flowers danced in the fields, primrose and poppy nodding and bowing in warm breezes that stirred the new-green grass. Birds busied themselves with nest-building and sang gloriously for joy of that soft spring that blessed the land, and noble notes of birdsong rang through the rows and ranks of blossoming wildwood.

Then came summer with warm winds, the breath of Zephyrus bearing boon for both man and beast. The land flourished and was fruitful and fair to see. Long days lingered, for the sun loved to shine upon such beauty, and there was time for to-ing and fro-ing in fellowship among men. But then the season rushed toward harvest time and the weather waxed hard, warning all nature to hurry toward ripeness before winter. Rough winds of heaven wrestled with the sun, and leaves were torn from the trees and tossed upon the earth. And the grass which was green before now was sere, and roses ripened and died. Thus passed the year in many yesterdays, and winter wended its way again as the world requires, until Michaelmas month came round with last winter's wager. And now Gawain began to think upon his anxious journey.

However, All Saints' Day he lingered with Arthur and he made a joyful occasion of the feast for the sake of his friends, with great revel and mirth at the Round Table. All the best of that company were gathered: Iwain, and Erik were there; and Sir Dodinel Le Sauvage, with his cousin Galeshin, the Duke of Clarence; and, son of King Ban of Benwick, the great Lancelot, and his cousin Lionel; and Lucan, that good man who served as Arthur's butler; and Sir Bors and Sir Bedivere, the hugest men of all the court; and the famed Mador de la Port. All were full of concern for the young man, but they allowed no sadness to show, no sign of worry, but only happiness and good will. And they made jests and joked though little joy was in their hearts.

After dinner Gawain turned to his uncle and spoke straightforwardly of his journey.

"My liege, I must ask leave of you. You know the nature of my undertaking, and I am bound for the quest on the morrow, to seek the Green Knight, with God as my help."

All the court gathered around to give counsel and cheer to the young knight, and the concern in their hearts was now clear on their faces. There was much sorrow in that chamber that so worthy and beloved a man as Gawain should set forth

on such a task, to perform such a dreadful deed with only his sword to aid him. But Gawain spoke cheerfully.

"Why should I be afraid? What can a man do but seek out his fate, be it fair or foul? What can a man do but try?"

In the morning he rose with the sun to prepare himself. He sent his man for clothes and armor and his groom to make ready his great white steed, Gringolet. First a richly patterned rug of finest tapestry wool was laid on the floor and all of his gleaming gear was spread out on it. Gawain bent down and selected a weapon and weighed it in his hands. He looked over all the battle gear, rubbing his hands over gleaming steel and testing the edge of sword and spear. Then he stood up and his man handed him a fine silken doublet which he slipped on, and then a skillfully made tunic of Cappadocian leather, snug at neck and trimmed with ermine. He put on the sabatons that covered his feet with metal, broad at the toe and with a leather sole, and he lapped his legs in steel greaves. The poleyns that covered his knees had been polished to a gleam and were fastened with knots of gold. Then the cuisses enclosed his brawny thighs and were tied with thongs, and a lined hauberk of bright steel rings was put on him, and burnished steel braces upon both arms with shining elbow pieces, and gauntlets of flexible metal, and all the gear that would stand him in good stead. Then the coat-armor, the heavy silken mantle embroidered with the devices of heraldry, was fastened at his neck, and it lay across his shoulders lightly and fell to the floor in shining folds. His golden spurs were fastened with pride and his sword was girt to his side by a silk sash.

When he was finally clasped within his armor, he was a splendid sight.

Each smallest knot gleamed with gold. Encased as he was, he went to the chapel to make his offering and to honor God at the high altar. Then he went to king and court to take leave of his liege and the lords and ladies. They kissed him and gave him over into the protection of God.

By this time Gringolet was ready, girt with a saddle gleaming gaily with gold fringe and glistening studs. The bridle was trimmed with braided gold and the breast-trappings and saddle skirt, crupper and coverlet, all matched the saddle bows. Everything was a rich red in color and decorated with gold nails that shone in the sun.

Then Gawain took up his helmet and put it on his head and fastened it firmly. It was heavily padded inside and so sat high on his head and clasped behind, with a thin silk scarf called a horson wound around it, embroidered with bright parrots preening, and doves, and true-love knots as thickly as if seven maids had sewn seven winters in its making. The gold circlet that embraced his temples was set with diamonds.

Then they brought forth his shield. It had a bright red background with a pentangle depicted on it in pure gold. Gawain seized it by the baldric and hung it upon his shoulder. Now the reason for that pentangle decorating the shield of this noble prince I shall tell you, even though it delay me.

It is a design that has five points and each side overlaps and links with another, and everywhere it is without end. The pentangle is a symbol that Solomon established long ago in token of truth and honor and pledged word. It is a symbol of perfection in heart and soul, and some people believe that it has the power to repel evil spirits. Therefore it is especially suitable for Gawain, for he was ever faithful, godly and pure, void of any villainy and virtuous in all things. Therefore he bore the pentangle on his shield and mantle as the truest and gentlest knight one could name. For Gawain was virtuous in five ways, and in each way in five things.

First, Gawain was faultless in his five senses. His eyesight was so keen that he was called "May-hawk," and in all other senses he was as excellent. Second, he never failed in the strength of his five fingers. And he meditated often upon the five wounds of Christ, and he celebrated the five joys of the Queen of Heaven. He had her likeness painted inside his shield at the top, so that when his gaze fell upon her face his courage was unwavering. In this he was like his uncle, for

Arthur carried the image of the Virgin into battle many times and always did it call her into his memory. And the fifth side of the pentangle represented Gawain's knightly virtues: generosity of soul, loving fellowship with all living things, purity, courtesy that never failed, and compassion that surpassed any point. These five qualities were more certainly found in Gawain than in any other. They girded him about like a shield, this man, each interlocked and fastened upon five points that never failed, without beginning or end. Therefore on his red shield was shaped the endless knot, that pure pentangle of folklore, shining with rich gold.

Now Gawain was ready and he grasped his lance lightly, and, turning away his face, he touched his steed with spurs and sprang on his way so speedily that sparks shot from the steel-clad hooves. Everyone who saw this sight was sick at heart and in their concern they spoke among themselves.

"It is too bad, by Christ! that that boy should be lost who is so noble!"

"To find his like again upon this earth will not be easy."

"He should have been more cautious and he might have become a duke."

"Yes, a brilliant leader of men in this land he could have been, and would better have been than to be destroyed for nothing, beheaded by a monster for his unguarded word."

"Whoever heard of a king to take such counsel in conference over a Christmas game!"

And many were the hot tears that bathed their eyes when that handsome man fared forth on that fateful day. Gawain wasted no time, however, but sped on his errand, and many a wilsome way he went, indeed.

Chapter IV

NOW he rode through the countryside far south of the Humber River, directed only by God, and it was no game to him. All alone, he passed that first cold night without comfort or companion. He had no friend but his horse as they traveled hills and woods, nor any but God with whom to keep company. After many weary days he came near to North Wales, and as he rode he kept the Isles of Anglesey always at the left. He wandered across the streams near the promontory at Holy Head and then into the wilderness of Wirral. Little there for either man or God to love! And everywhere as he roamed he inquired of the folk if they had heard mention of a green knight or of a green chapel in any area thereabout. All answered him nay, that never in their lives had they seen or heard of any man of that hue.

So Gawain took many a strange road over many a dreary hillside, searching this way and that, but no green chapel could he find. Many a cliff he climbed in the rough countryside as he wandered, far from friends. A stranger he rode. At each riverside he found before him a foe, a ferocious enemy foul and fell, that he must fight. And he found so many marvels among the mountains that it would be difficult to tell the tenth of it. Sometimes he struggled with dragons or wolves, sometimes with the trolls who lived among the crags, or with wild bulls and bears and boars, or with the giants who pursued him through the high rocks. Had he not been courageous and steadfast and committed to keep his word, doubtless he would soon have been dead.

But the fighting affected him less than the weather, for it had become much worse. Cold rain shivered from the gray skies and froze before it could hit the pale earth. Soaked with cold sleet and nearly dead, he slept on bare rocks in his armor more nights than enough as the cold showers thundered down from the mountaintop or hung high over his head in heavy icicles. Thus in peril and pain and terrible plight the poor man rode through the land until Christmas Eve, and as he rode, he prayed to the Goddess of Heaven that she might direct his steps and guide him to some safe haven.

He rode past a mountain into forest deep and dark, with hills on each side and heavy woods of ancient oaks by the hundreds. The hazel and the hawthorn grew there together with rough ragged moss spreading everywhere, and many an unblithe bird shivered upon bare twig, piping piteously for pain of the cold. The man on Gringolet glided beneath them through mist and murk, one man all alone, worried that he could not say his service to his Lord who had been born on this very night to bear our burdens. As he rode, seeking everywhere a suitable place, he prayed, "I beseech you, Lord, and also you, Mary, mother mild, for some lodging where I might observe Mass and your matins on the morrow. Meekly I ask, and to that end I now pray my "Pater" and my "Ave" and "Credo." He prayed continuously and he wept for his failing and then he crossed himself three times.

Hardly had he done this when suddenly he became aware of a moated castle in the distance near a wood on a green lawn rising to a knoll surrounded by the boughs of many large trees lining the moat. The fairest castle, surely, that any knight might see, set in a meadow, a park all about, with a peaked palisade two miles around enclosing it. Gawain contemplated that stronghold as it shimmered among the white oaks. Then he took off his helmet and thanked God who had shown him such mercy and hearkened to his cries.

"Still, I must ask hospitality here," he said to himself, and he touched Gringolet with golden spur and rode toward the main gate leading to the drawbridge. The bridge itself was drawn shut, the gate was locked fast. The walls were sturdy and feared no blast of wind or bugle.

Gawain waited there on the bank of the deep ditch which enclosed the place. The wall stood in the water wonderfully deep, and its full height of hard-hewn stone reared up to the heavens. There were many turrets, with great windows that overlooked the land in all directions. A better barbican Gawain had never looked upon. Further in he could see a high hall between the towers, with thick trochets, high pinnacles that fitted together cunningly, with carved ornamental tops worked with fine craft. He saw chalk-white chimneys on the gleaming roofs of the towers. So many painted pinnacles were scattered everywhere among the castle's embrasures, clustered so thickly, that they seemed, in the cold blue light of the sky, to have been cut out of paper. The young knight thought that it would be a fine thing if he could come within that dwelling and harbor in that pleasant shelter through the holiday.

He called out, and soon a smiling porter came to the wall to greet the wandering knight and to inquire of his errand.

"Good sir," said Gawain politely, "I ask hospitality here. Will you take my request to the lord of this house?"

"Yea," said the porter, "and I can assure you, sir, that you will be welcome to stay here as long as you like."

Then he came down quickly, and many others came with him to welcome the visitor. They let down the huge gate and came out and knelt down on the cold earth to greet this noble knight. Gawain bid them rise, and they yielded him the broad gate, set it wide open before him, and Gawain rode over the bridge into the fine courtyard. There a groom took his bridle, and Gawain leaped down lightly as men took his horse to be stabled. When he raised his helmet a man sprang forth to take it from his hand, serving him eagerly, and another took his sword and shield. And the smiling knights and squires led him into the castle. Still in his fine raiment, he went into the hall where a brisk fire burned upon the hearth. There he greeted each person individually, and many a man pressed forward proudly to do him honor.

Then the castle's lord came forth from his chamber to meet, with all politesse, the man who had come.

"You are welcome to stay as long as you like, sir. All that is here is yours to have at whim or will."

"I thank you, sir," replied Gawain, "and ask God's blessing on you."

Thus they greeted each other with pleasure, these two, clasping arms in glad friendship's gesture.

Gawain looked at this man who so warmly greeted him and thought to himself that this was a bold knight indeed, this castle's owner, huge, and in the prime of life. He stood firm on legs solid as tree trunks; his face was serious, and ruddy as a fire; broad and beaverhued was his beard, and his speech was easy and bold. He seemed to Gawain very well suited to hold lordship over these good people.

The lord motioned a page forward and Gawain was led to a room, a bright bower where the bedding was regal, of soft silk with gold-embroidered hems, with coverlets made up of intricate panels, trimmed with bright ermine. Bed curtains were gathered on gold rings and held back by golden ropes, and tapestries of Toulouse silk and Tarsia fabric of the finest were laid out on the floor. Some knights, courteously curious, had accompanied him to the chamber, and they made many a comment about Gawain's mail shirt and his bright raiment as the attendants undressed him. Then rich garments were brought to him from which he could choose what he liked best, soft flowing clothes that slid silkenly over his young body, of colors so fresh and sweetly hued that it seemed Spring had suddenly made its appearance. All agreed that there had never been a handsomer, comelier knight, and that, wherever in the world he might have come from, he must surely be a prince without peer in any country of bold men.

When they returned to the great hall, a place was ready for Gawain before the hearth where a charcoal fire was burning. He sat upon cushions embroidered with strange devices. A bright mantle of brown silk, lined with soft fur, was thrown over his shoulders, and Gawain warmed himself and became cheerful. Soon a table was set up on trestles, covered with a clean white cloth, then with a fine overcloth, and saltcellars and silver spoons. A golden basin was brought and Gawain washed and then went to the table. He was served with several excellent stews seasoned in the best fashion, and many kinds of fish, some baked in a crust, some broiled on coals, some boiled, some stewed with spices and in skillful sauces, all prepared just as he liked. Freely and often Gawain called this a fine feast, and all the party encouraged him to enjoy himself at his pleasure. And they jested, saying that this was but poor fare, but soon it would improve. Gawain laughed with them, and joined in their light jokes, for the wine had gone to his head a little.

Then tactful inquiries were made about his circumstances and his background; discreet questions were put to the young prince, that they might know from what court he came. He told them that the gracious King Arthur held his allegiance, Arthur the royal king of the Round Table, and that it was Gawain himself who stood before them, come by the chance in this Christmas season.

The people were struck with amazement and joyous to learn his name for they knew that all excellence and skill was his, and his praise was in the mouths of all men on earth for his noble character and his honor. And they were glad that God had given them this goodly gift, the presence of Gawain in this court. Now, they said, we shall have report of noble manners and courtly behavior and example of chivalrous adventure, when a man of his high birth shall sit and sing with us.

And the lord of the castle laughed aloud, great bellows of laughter bursting from him when he learned what knight he was hosting in that holy time.

When dinner was done and the royal guest had risen, it was late nightfall and darkness drew around the castle. Chaplains began hurrying to the chapel's gate as they rightly should, and they rang the bells with right good will, calling all to evensong. The lord led the way, his lady beside him, into a pleasant little prayer room. And Gawain went happily along with them as the lord held his arm in the friendliest fashion and again cried warmest welcome in the world to him. Then they sat, sober and serious, through the simple service.

When they came out of the chapel, the lady began to cast glances at the knight. Gawain thought her the fairest of women, in shape and coloring, the fairest of all in song or story, even Guenevere, and as often as she looked at him, Gawain looked at her. Another lady held her by the left hand, one much older than she—an ancient, she seemed—but highly honored in this house, with handmaidens and attendants all about her. But the two ladies were very unlike to look upon, for the young one was fresh, while withered was the older. Rich rosy blushes colored the face of the one, while rough wrinkled cheeks hung in folds on the other. One had on bright kerchiefs with many precious pearls, her breast and throat bare to view, glowing whiter than the snow that gleams on the hillside. The other was covered with a white gorget over breast and throat, right up to her hairy chin, her bosom folded in silk, muffled up everywhere, and pinched and pleated with ruffles about so that nothing could be seen but the black brows, two burning eyes, a sharp nose, and thin, naked lips sour to see and smeared with grease. Her body was short and thick, her bottom broad and heavy. Surely more delicious to look upon was she who walked by her side!

Gawain took leave of his host and went over to that fair one who looked upon him so graciously. He greeted the older lady first, as custom requires, bowing low before her. The younger he took into his arms and he kissed her courteously and made all polite greetings, and declared himself to be their servant. They welcomed him warmly into their acquaintance and then, one on each side holding his arm, they led him to the main hall. At the hearthside they called for spiced mead and red wine. The gracious host leaped up often, thinking of good cheer and pleasure for his guest, and they shook off their mantles and hoods as the wine and the fire warmed them, and they devoted themselves to delight. With noisy laughter the lord made it a challenge to gladden Sir Gawain with games.

"I shall try, by my faith, to joust with word and wit, though I lose my shirt with the help of my friends." And all through the evening there were many games in the hall and shouted challenges and calls, with tests of skill and speed and surprise. Riot rang through the hall until it was late, and the host called it a night and Gawain finally took himself off to bed.

Chapter V

IN the morning, the birthday of the Lord who was to die for our destiny, good will filled each man in the world. So did it there among that fine company. Both at Mass and at meals everyone on floor or dais was dressed in his best, and the old crone sat in the highest place, the master of the castle at her side. Gawain, the lady, and the rest of the company sat together in the great hall as the dishes of food came, and throughout the room each man, at his proper degree of rank, was placed and served. There was food and drink and so much mirth that it is difficult to tell about. But I can say that Gawain and the fair lady took much pleasure in one another's company, in lighthearted trifling with smooth words, with fine courtly conversation—not unseemly in any way, you may be sure—as she played bantering games with the young prince. Trumpets and kettledrums made music through the room; each man minded his business and they minded theirs.

Great merriment continued the next day and the third, as days thronged together. At last the guests prepared to leave on the next morn, and so they stayed up late on that last night, and drank much wine and danced unceasingly to the singing of carols. When it was very late they took their leave, for on the dawn each would wend his long way home.

Gawain bid his host goodnight, but that man took him by the arm and led him to his own chamber and sat him down beside the hearth and thanked him heartily for the great honor that he had done to his home in that holy season.

"I am certain, Sir Gawain, that my reputation has grown great since Gawain has been my guest at God's own festival."

Gawain smiled and said, "Sir, I am beholden to you in all things, as courtesy commands, and will do your bidding at your behest; but truly, all honor is yours already, as God grants it."

The host tried hard to persuade Gawain to remain for a longer time, but Gawain responded that he could not. Then he inquired what dire deed had driven Gawain from the king's court at that special time, to go off on his own before the holiday greenery had been removed from the halls.

"Truly, sir," Gawain said, "it is as you have said. An important mission, and a pressing one, called me from my home, for I am required to seek a place which I do not know where to find in all this world. I only know that I must come upon it on New Year's day somewhere, with God's help.

"Can you tell me, sir, if you have ever heard of a green chapel, or where it might be, or of the knight who lives there, a man the very color of green? A vow was made between us. I must meet that man at that place on this New Year that now draws near. And I would look upon that man, if God will permit it, more gladly than upon any other. Therefore, I must ask your leave to depart your house, for I have barely three days, and I would as soon be doomed to death as to fail in this mission."

Then said the smiling host, "Linger here a little longer, friend, for I can direct you to that appointed place. Let the green chapel in the woods bother you no more, for you may be in your bed at your ease for four days and travel on the first of the year and come to that place by midmorning to do whatever you must do there. So stay here, my friend, through New Year's day and rise and depart then. My man shall start you on your way—it is not two miles hence."

Then Gawain was very relieved and laughed happily, "Now I thank you heartily for this, above all other things. Now that my purpose is achieved, I shall surely remain here at your will and do whatever you ask."

Then they clasped hands and sat together as friends and the host sent for the ladies and other knights to cheer them even more. There was sweet solace, indeed! And the lord was so noisy with mirth and merriment that he seemed like a man taken leave of his wits. He leaped up often, fetching food and wine, and then called out to Gawain, shouting loudly, "You have, I remind you, promised to do my bidding. Do you hold to that vow here and now?"

"Certainly," said the true knight, "for while I abide beneath your roofbeams I am bound to your bidding."

"Then, go to your rest. I know you have traveled from afar and here you have stayed up late with me, and surely you are not recovered in strength and sleep. So tomorrow stay in bed and rest at your ease. Come to breakfast when you will, and my wife here shall sit with you and comfort you with her company until I return to the castle. Tomorrow I rise early to go hunting and shall be gone until dark."

Gawain agreed to all this, as he must.

"That out of the way," continued his host, "let us make a little wager. Whatsoever I gain tomorrow in the woods shall be yours, and whatsoever fortune may hand you, you will turn over to me. So we shall swap the day's spoils, and let us so swear, whether the prize turn out to be worthless or better."

"Bigod," laughed Gawain, "I see you like to amuse yourself. Indeed, I agree to it!"

"Then let's drink to it. The bargain is made!"

They clasped hands and then they laughed and drank and the evening passed in polite games and many courtly courtesies until each took his leave. With much light laughter each man was lighted to his bed with flickering torches, but before they parted the terms of that agreement were again discussed. The lord of that castle knew very well how to make a high jest!

Chapter VI

ERY EARLY, before sunrise, everyone got up, and those guests who were leaving called for their grooms and got their horses saddled up, their gear ready, packed their bags, and dressed in their finest clothing, to ride out fully arrayed. Mounting up and seizing the bridle, each guest went his own way.

The liege lord of that land was not the last readied for riding. He ate a bite hastily, said his prayers, and called his company together. With the blast of a bugle they rushed off to the hunting fields, and by the time the sun shone full upon the earth, he and his companions were away on their mounts.

Then the cacheres, the dog-handlers who took care of the hounds, unlocked the kennels and called forth the dogs, blowing the three long notes of the bare-mote lustily upon the horns. The small scenting beagle hounds bayed fiercely and made a rough noise, and the grooms shouted and cracked whips and hurried to head off those dogs that had gone dashing wildly around. And there were fully a hundred hunters, I have heard, of the very best. The vewters, keepers of the deer hounds, went off to their appointed hunting stations and cast off the hunting leashes, and as the hounds broke away, great blasts of the horns shredded the silence of that forest.

At first utterance of the baying hounds, the wild wood quaked. Deer fled through the hollows, mad with fear, rushing to the high ground, only to be turned back by the ring of beaters who shouted loudly. The beaters let the harts, with their high tossing antlers, find an escape, and the bright bucks with their broad horns; for the lord had decreed that in this season no man might molest any male deer. The hinds were hauled in with cries of "Heigh!" and " 'ware," and the does were driven with great din into the deep valleys. There one could see, as the deer slipped by, the glitter of flashing arrows. At each turn in the wood an arrow awaited, thudding into the broad brown heads, and the deer screamed and bled and died there on the broad banks, as the hounds pursued them closely and hunters with loud blasts of the horns hurried after them with echoing cries that seemed to crack the cliffs. They were harried and driven from the high land, harassed to stand at bay on the creeksides. Whatever beast escaped the hunters' arrows was pulled down and torn apart at the killing stations. The men were so skillful at their work and the greyhounds so ferocious that they seized upon the deer quickly and brought them down faster than the eye could take in. The master was carried away with excitement, dashing and galloping about, jumping off and on his horse, shouting and cursing and laughing aloud. So passed the day with pleasure until evening drove on.

Thus the lord amused himself in the borders of the woods, and Gawain, that gentle knight, lay in his bed, lingering while the sun gleamed on the walls, under a silken coverlet, the bed curtains drawn about him. As he lay, half dreaming, he thought he heard a little sound at the door, and he raised his head and peeked out warily to see what it might be.

The lady it was!—fair to look upon, who closed the door softly behind her and came toward the bed. Gawain lay down quickly and pretended to be asleep, and she stole over and lifted up the curtain and crept within and sat down lightly on the bedside, and watched until he should awaken. Gawain lay lurked a long while, mulling over in his mind as to what might be the circumstances, moved to wonder, to marvel even. But he said to himself, "It would be more seemly to give over this pretense and to seek to discover with polite speech what this lady may want." And so he awakened and stirred and turned toward her and opened his eyes and looked about, and he crossed himself, as if by his prayers the safer to be.

With cheeks sweetly pink and looking lovely in truth, the lady smiled upon him with laughing red lips.

"Good morning, Sir Gawain," she said lightly. "You are an unwary sleeper, that one may creep up on you so. Now are you taken by surprise! But let us call a truce, and I shall bind you in your bed to make sure of you." Thus the laughing lady cast her jests.

"Good morning, fair one," replied Gawain blithely. "I find myself at your service and under your will, and that suits me well. I yield myself eagerly and cry quits. And that is the most I can do." So he jested easily, and laughed as he spoke. Then he sat up. "But allow me to rise and dress, fair captor, that I may more comfortably converse with you."

"No, indeed," she responded firmly. "I will not rise from your bed, I can assure you, but rather will keep you here in my power. You can do your talking from this spot. For I hold here the famed Gawain, whom all the world worships wherever he may ride. Your honor, your courtliness are praised, both by lords and by ladies." She smiled at this, her white teeth gleaming, and her eyes shone with pleasure at the game in her grasp. "And now you are here, and I am here, and we are alone. My husband and his men are off on a lengthy hunt, and the others, even my maids, are still abed. The door is shut and bolted with its hasp. And since I have under my roof the man most admired by the whole world, I shall take advantage of the time while it lasts."

She leaned closer, her white arms reaching, her eyes holding his. "Come, you are welcome to my arms, your own to take. I relinquish my power and put myself under your command."

"Truly, my dear," responded Gawain, "I cannot possibly be the man you speak of. I am not worthy of these kind attentions, I know that. But I thank you for the good thought, and if I were so worthy, to set myself to your pleasure, ah, that would be pure joy."

"Nay, sire, I know you, and it would be discourteous for me to take lightly your excellence and prowess in these skills. For there are plenty of ladies who would rather have you in their grasp, as I have you here, to dally with your courtly words and let go of all cares and to find comfort with you, than to have the world's treasures and gold. And, as I love that great Lord who holds up the heavens, here I have, through His grace, that which they all desire."

Thus she cozened him so cleverly, that lady fair of face, that Gawain could only answer, with cautious speech, everything that she said.

"Madam, may that Lord grant you grace, and I thank you for your noble generosity; certainly these folk you speak of regard my deeds too highly, and I do not deserve such devotion. It is only your kindness that sees naught but good."

"Sir, I cannot agree. For were I worth all the host of women alive, and were all the riches of the world in my hand, and I could pick and choose from among all men, from what I know of you, dear man, of beauty and gentle breeding and fine wit, which I have only heard of before but now know to be true, then of all men there would be none chosen over you, my dear."

"Indeed," he replied, "you could have chosen better, madam. But I am proud of the favor that you bestow upon me and I pledge myself to be your knight."

Thus they bandied words, speaking of such things as the morning passed, and ever the lady showed that she loved him greatly. But Gawain fenced with her carefully and acquitted himself well. And the lady thought to herself, even if I were the fairest of women, I could not arouse love in his heart. She knew that his mind was on his journey and the fate he must face, and would be until the deed was done.

So, glancing at him, she laughed, and rising, she astonished him with sharp words.

"Now I see that I must give you this game. But I can scarcely believe that you are Gawain."

"Why?" he asked, fearful that he had failed in the formalities of his rank.

"So great a knight as Gawain, the living example of courtesy, could never have lingered so long with a lady without claiming a kiss, or at least hinting of it by some trifling remark in speech."

"Then let it be as you wish, madam. I shall kiss at your command, as it is a knight's duty. And, as I would never displease you, say no more."

She came to him then, and caught him in her arms and leaned down and kissed him lightly. So they took their fond farewell and she went out the door without another word, and Gawain leaped from the bed and that right quickly!

He called his chamberlain and selected his clothes and when he was dressed, he went to the chapel. And then he sat down to the meal which the servants had kept ready for him and made merry with games at the court all day, until the moonrise. There was never so comely a knight to be found, amusing the two royal ladies through the day. They all applied themselves to pleasure.

Chapter VII

NOW the lord of the land was also having his games, hunting in hold and heath in the hind's domain. So many he slew there of does and other deer that it is a wonder to tell. Hunters hurried to the killing ground and made a quick quarry of the quelled deer. Men experienced in the task selected the choicest animals and butchered them in the proper manner. And even the smallest deer bore two fingers' width of fat meat.

They made the first cut and pulled out the upper stomach. They emptied it and scraped it and knotted up the fat within it. Then they removed the skin from the four legs and broke open the belly and took out the bowels and discarded them. They grasped the throat of the deer and separated weasand from windpipe and took out the guts. Then they cut out the meat of the shoulders with sharp knives, slicing with small strokes to have whole sides. They carved the breast down the middle and with a quick stroke ripped it down right to the fork of the legs. And here they cut into the folds of skin, slicing it to loosen the meat from the bone. So with skilled hand and sharp knife they cleared all the backbone down to the haunches and pulled all the meat loose in one piece. Then the head was hewed off, and the ravens' fee was thrown into a thicket, as ritual requires. Then they pierced each thick side near the ribs and hung the meat by a leather thong from a tree branch, each man taking his allotted share. On a piece of hide they placed the dogs' portion—the liver and lights, the tripes, all mingled with bread and soaked in the blood.

Then proudly they blew the "prize," the dogs bayed and

howled, and they gathered up all the meat and turned homeward, sounding stout notes on strong horns. By sunset all the company had returned to the castle where Gawain had been all that day, taking his pleasure beside the brightly burning fire. The lord came to him there and cheer and good will filled that chamber.

The lord commanded all to gather, the ladies and knights, and when they had done so, he bid his men fetch the venison, and in the spirit of the game, he called Gawain and displayed to him the tally sticks of all the deer slain and showed him the fine meat which he had won.

"How can you equal this prize?" he asked, and he laughed and clapped Gawain's shoulder. "Through skillful craft of hunting I have earned all this!"

"Indeed," said Gawain, "here is certainly the finest game meat that I've seen in seven years of winter."

"And I give it all to you, Gawain, for by our agreement you can claim it as your own."

"That is true," Gawain replied, "and I say the same to you: what I have won here today belongs to you, and I yield it with good will." And he clasped his fine host with his arms and kissed him heartily. "Take you therefore my winnings; I gained nothing else. And if it were ten times more I would grant it as freely."

"I thank you for that, and in good faith I take my due. But be that as it may, I'd like to know where you took this prize, and whether by your own wits or another's."

But Gawain laughed. "No, sir, that was not our bargain. Press me no more, for you have received all you are entitled to!" And they laughed together then in friendship and off to supper they went.

Servants brought wine to them often as they sat at hearthside in the great hall and they repeated their contract made the day before, to exchange all their winnings, whatever chance might bring, when they met again at night. This covenant they reaffirmed before all the court, and jesting toasts were made by the laughing lords and ladies. It grew late and they separated with affectionate words, each man hastening to his bed.

As soon as the cock had crowed the lord leaped out of bed calling for his servants. Meat and mass were quickly finished, and the company dressed for the hunt ere the sun had risen, and they were off to the chase. Unleashed braches ran and raced through the thorn thickets and loud were the horns and "halloos" of the hunt as they poured over the open fields.

Soon the call for the quest sounded from the marsh and the hunters rallied to the dogs who had given first voice. The hounds, hearing the hunters, raced to their sides, dashing, tongues lolling, fast to the trail, forty at a time. Such a baying and blaring of the assembling dogs arose that the rocks rang with their barking. Hunters urged them on with horn and loud cries. Then in one merging mass, they rushed together between a pool in the creek and an overhanging crag. Over a wooded hill by the cliff at the edge of the marsh where heavy boulders had fallen in tumbled heaps, the dogs kept the trail, the men pelting after them. They cast about the gnarled crags and the woods, all certain that the beast, whose presence was announced by the circling dogs, lay hidden nearby. They beat the bushes and called on the creature to come forth.

Suddenly, without warning he burst out, seeking his tormentors. The most gigantic swine—a marvelous sight!—shot out of the bushes, a boar who had been growing to this huge size through many years. And he was fierce, a grim, grunting monster who brought grief to many, for he brought down three dogs at that first rush and would harm many more that day. The men shouted and cursed and blew blasts on the horn, recalling the hounds from the heart of the fray. Then wild were their cries and the yelps of the hounds that chased after the boar with baleful baying. Often the old boar stopped to face the pack, maiming a dog or two in the melee, before dashing off headlong, and the wounded hounds howled pitifully in their pain. The bowmen ran up to shoot at the boar, and they got off many arrows, hitting him often. But the barbs bounced off the thick hide of his shoulders, and the points could not pierce his thick skin, and the shafts splintered to pieces. But many blows brought pain and suddenly, maddened by battle, he rushed the men who encircled him. Many were hurt, and they fell back, afraid, and some fled in fear. But the lord, on his light horse, galloped after, blowing his bugle, sounding the rallying cry, tearing through the thick brush, pursuing the boar closely as the sun climbed the sky.

In this fashion the lord occupied his time in the field while our noble lad lay in his comfortable bed at home. The lady did not forget him; she was at him early, to catch him off guard and alter his heart.

She lifted up the curtain and peeked in at the knight. Gawain welcomed her at once, and she gave him honeyed words and sat softly by his side and smiled often. But soon, with a teasing look, she said,

"If you are indeed Gawain, I think it is very strange that a man so widely known for his perfection in knighthood does not know the proper observances of polite society. If anyone seeks to school you in courtesy, you cast off such lessons from your mind. You have already forgotten that just yesterday I wooed you with the warmest words I could."

"What are you saying?" said Gawain in surprise. "Indeed, I do not understand. If what you say is true, certainly the blame is mine."

"Yet I taught you about kissing," said the fair one, "and that the custom is to claim the token quickly. Any worthy knight understands this courtesy."

"That is hard speech, my lady, for you know that I dare not ask lest I be refused. If I were rejected, I would indeed have erred in taking the risk."

"In faith," said the laughing lady, "you know very well that you would not be refused. And if anyone should be so discourteous as to refuse you, certainly you are strong enough to obtain by force whatsoever you might desire."

"Ah, no, madam, in my country force does no honor to the user and unlucky is the gift which is not given freely and with good will. I am at your command, to kiss when you like. You may do as you choose and cease when you wish."

And the lady bent down and kissed his face and then they settled down to speak of all manner of things. But she soon turned the talk to her heart's desire.

"I would know more about you," said the noble lady, "if you promise not to get angry. What is the riddle of one so young, and yet so valiant, so courteous and knightly as you are known to be? Of all the arts of chivalry, the chief things praised are skill at the true sport of love and the science of knightly warfare. For when the deeds of true knights are told, the title and text of their deeds is how these lads ventured their lives for love of their ladies, dared and endured much for their love, avenged them with valor and freed them from sorrows, and brought joy to their hearts with virtuous acts. And of all knight-errantry, you are the finest. Your reputation and respect are widespread. And here I have sat at your side twice now and never have I heard words of love, no, not one. Surely you, so eager and earnest in your vows of knighthood, should yearn to show a young maiden some sign of your skill.

"Can it be that you are stupid? You who are the center of all this fame? Or perhaps you deem me too dull to indulge your dalliance? You do not wish to waste your wit on one so unworthy?

"For shame! I have come here alone, to sit by your side, to learn of your skill. Come, teach me, while my husband is still far from home."

"By my soul," cried Gawain, "God knows my delight in this dalliance is huge, and great is my joy at this game! To think that so worthy a maiden would come to me here and trouble herself with so unworthy a man as I affords me the purest pleasure. But to undertake to speak of true love or to teach the texts of chivalrous tales to you who, I know very well, have more skill in the art than a hundred like me—this indeed were manifold folly! But command me, my lady, and

I will do your bidding as best I can, for I am beholden and will always seek to serve you, with God's help."

In this way she tested and tempted him in order to win him to sin, whatever else she might have had in mind. But Gawain defended himself so cleverly that there seemed no fault, nor was there any evil on either side, and they exchanged nothing but joy. They laughed and chatted a long while, and at last she kissed him, took her gracious leave and went her way. And Gawain rose and dressed and met the ladies at breakfast, and all day they amused themselves.

But the lord of the castle galloped over the fields pursuing the boar as he rushed along the riverbanks. Often he stood at bay and broke the backs of the best hounds, but as often the bowmen attacked and drove him from safety willy-nilly, to turn and run from the hurtful arrows. Nevertheless he made the staunchest men fall back until at last he was so exhausted that he could run no longer. He made for a hole in the rocks near the riverbank where a stream bubbled. He got the bank at his back and began to snort and paw the ground. Froth foamed from his ugly snout and flecked the wicked tusks. The boldest warriors hesitated, fearful of drawing too near, and they hung back from danger. Who could call them coward? He had already inflicted so much hurt that they were loath to risk those sharp white tusks.

Then the master himself came, urging his horse forward, and he saw the boar at bay, his men helpless before him. At once he leaped from his horse and, dropping the reins, he drew a shining sword. He strode forward, pushing through the underbrush with broad shoulders until he reached the waiting beast. The animal was wary of this man with a weapon in his hand, and his bristles stiffened and he snorted and grunted fiercely. The watching men were fearful lest their lord should be killed.

The boar rushed out to meet the man and they two were a twisting, grappling heap splashing in the shallow water of the creek. As they met head on, the boar had the worst of it, for the man managed to get in the first blow. He drove the sharp steel deep into the boar's throat, and again, up to the hilt. At last he pierced the heart and the bright blood burst from the body. Still snarling, the boar rolled over in the bloody burn and gave up the struggle. The men dragged him to a grassy bank where a hundred hounds set upon him and brought quick and certain death.

Then there was the blowing of the "prize" on many a gleaming horn, a high "hallo"-ing shouted by the men. The braches, who had been the chief hunters of the pell-mell chase, bayed their triumph. Then one of the men skilled in the craft began to cut up the huge animal. First he hewed off the head and stuck it on a stake. Then he cut along the shaggy backbone and separated the two halves, and drew out the innards to reward the dogs. He cut the meat in broad, thick slabs and burned the entrails on the coals of the fire. He fastened the two halves together and hung the carcass on a strong staff. With their prize they headed toward home, the boar's head carried before the man who had killed it with his own hands.

When he saw Sir Gawain in the great hall, he shouted out for him to come and see what his fee for that day would be. He roared with laughter and there was much excited talk. The good ladies were called in and gathered around. He showed them the prize and shaped for them the scope and length of the hunt, the ferocity of the battle with the wild boar as it fled through the woods. Gawain praised the deed and the prize obtained. Such a brawn of a beast, a swine of such size, said he, he never had seen! They all handled the head and Gawain expressed horror for the danger faced.

"Ah now, Gawain, this game is yours, as you know by our agreement."

"True, and as freely do I give you all my day's gain." And he seized the lord by the collar and kissed him heartily twice.

"Now are we even," he said.

"By Saint Giles," laughed the lord ruefully, "you are the best! At this rate of trading, you will be rich before long!"

Then tables were set up and covered with white cloths. Bright light from the waxen torches danced on the walls. Men sat and were served all through the room and joy leaped up like the fire in the fireplace and all was pleasure. Afterwards there were songs and dances and all the mannerly mirth that men may tell.

And ever the lovely lady kept our young knight close by her side. Such attention she paid to him, sly smiles and secret looks, seeking to please him, that Gawain was all forwondered and beguiled, and even somewhat angry. He could not, for fear of offense, refuse her attentions, but he dealt with her in careful courtesy, uneasy in his mind.

When all had eaten and drunk to their heart's desire, the lord called Gawain to him and they went to his chamber and settled down at the fireside. There they drank and joked and soon the lord suggested that again they keep to their bargain on the next day, which would be the New Year's eve. Gawain, however, craved permission to leave in the morning, for the time now drew nigh when he must face his fate. Soon or late, each man must dree his wyrd as God has decreed. But again his host dissuaded him from that and urged him to remain.

"As I am an honorable man, I promise that you shall make your way to the Green Chapel to take care of your business on the New Year's day, long before the sun has reached mid-sky. Therefore, do you lie abed and take your ease, and I shall tomorrow hunt in the holt, and exchange with you the day's profit, whatever it may be. For I have twice tested you and found you true, but three times makes the trial. So tomorrow let us make merry while we may, our minds on happiness; for a man who seeks sorrow may find it easily enough."

Gawain could not refuse to grant his host's request and they stayed up until, dazzled with drink, they were lighted to their beds. Gawain slept soundly all night and late into morning, but the lord was up early to pursue his hunting plans.

Chapter VIII

FTER MASS, he and his men took a morsel of food.
Bright-shining was the morning as he called for
his mount. All of the men who were going on the hunt were
mounted up and waiting for him at the castle gates. Fair was
the countryside where the frost still clung. The sun rose
against blushing clouds floating across the morning sky.

The hunters unleashed their hounds near the edge of the
woods and the rocks rang with the sound of the horns. Some
of the dogs fell upon the trail of the fox, traversing the criss-
cross path that the fox, with skill of cunning practice, had
made. A small kennet sounded the cry and the hunt was called
on him. The other dogs rushed to follow the one who had
first caught the scent, running forth in a rushing rabble after
the track, and he frisked along ahead. Soon they caught sight
of the fox. Men cried the "view hallo!" when they saw him,
and the dogs pursued closely, denouncing him loudly with
angry barks. The fox twisted and turned through many a
rough grove, doubling back and stopping often by the hedges
to listen. Then he leaped over a thorn hedge that ran along
a little spinney, and he stole out quietly to the edge of a small
woods. He had almost escaped the hounds by his cleverness,
but before he knew it, he blundered suddenly into a hunting
station, where three fierce greyhounds set upon him at once.
He swerved quickly away and dashed off in a new direction,
fleeing to the woods for fear of his life.

Then it was brave sport indeed to hear the hounds sounding together, as the whole pack converged upon him. Such a
tempest they raised round his head that it sounded as if all
the surrounding cliffs had clattered down in a heap. Loudly

was he cried when the men caught sight of him; eagerly was he met with the snarling voices of the hounds. Like a thief he was chased, the harriers always at his tail, so that he could not tarry even to take a breath. Often he ran out to face the attack, and as often he retreated, so wily was Reynard. And always he led them by devious ways, that lord and his men, round and round in merry chase while the sun climbed to midday and the young knight slept contentedly at home within the silken curtains on that cold morning.

But the lady for love could not sleep, nor was she weakened in the purpose that burned in her heart. She rose up early, wrapped herself in a long mantle, one that was lined and collared with fur, and she wrapped scarves like bright jewels around her hair. Her glowing face and brow were bare, her breast and shoulders too. She came within the chamber door and closed it softly after. She opened a window and called to the young man, greeting him with loving words. "Ah, man, how can you sleep so on such a bright morning?"

He was deep in direful dreams, but even so, he sensed that she was near. In the heavy gloom of those dark dreams he muttered and mumbled, as a man may who is troubled with tortured thought. Destiny that day would deal him his wyrd at the Green Chapel where he was to meet the green man and bear his blow without debate or delay. But when the maiden came, he recovered his wits and responded as quickly as he could. She came to him with sweet smiles, and she bent over his fair face and kissed him gently. He welcomed her graciously with honest pleasure. He saw her, so glorious and so gaily attired, so faultless in feature and complexion so clear that joy welled up and warmed his heart. With smooth sweet smiling they languished in the happiness and bliss that was between them; they uttered sweet words and took much delight in each other. But great was the peril that shadowed them, unless Heaven should rescue this knight.

The proud princess pressed him so eagerly, urged him so near the breaking point that he was forced either to yield to her love or churlishly refuse. He was concerned for his courtesy lest he should appear to be craven, but also for disaster to himself lest he should commit a sin and be a traitor to the man whose hospitality he enjoyed. He said to himself, God grant that I should not fall; and with light love-laughter he parried all the teasing speeches that fell from her honeyed lips.

She said, "Blame before all the world shall be your reward if you do not love the woman who, wounded in heart, lies next to you. Unless you have a lover already whom you like better, and you wish to remain faithful to that one, bound so tightly by your vows that you cannot break the chains—and that I cannot believe! But if so, tell me now, I pray you. For all the love in the world, do not deceive me with guile."

Gawain smiled gently and said, "By St. John, truly I have no love, my lady, nor shall I for a while."

"Those are surely the worst words of all," she replied, "but I am answered truthfully, the worse for me. But kiss me now and I shall take comfort from that; for I must mourn through all my days in this world as do many other lovers." Sighing, she bent down and kissed him, and then drew back from him, and as she stood she said, "Now, beloved, at this our parting do me a favor. Give me some small token, a gift, your glove perhaps, that I may keep by me to lessen my sadness."

Gawain said, "I wish I had here the most precious thing in life to give you for your love, for truly you have deserved more reward than I might reckon. But to give you a love-token would avail but little, for it would not honor you to have a keepsake of mine. I am on a fearful errand and carry no hoard of precious things. I am sorry, lady, and it shames me greatly. But a man must do what he must, accepting his fate without plaint or repine."

"Well, my lord of high honor, even though I may have nothing of yours, you shall have something of mine."

She pulled from her finger a rich ring worked of red gold set with a dazzling stone which shone in the sun. You may be sure it was worth a good deal of money, and she pressed it on him. But Gawain refused it.

"I will accept no gifts, my lady, for I have none to give you now."

But she urged him eagerly, though he refused her repeatedly and swore by his honor that he would take nothing. She was pained that he would deny her.

"If you refuse this ring because it seems too rich and you would not be so beholden, I shall give you my girdle, which is not worth much."

And she unfastened a small knot of ribbon which held the girdle-scarf around her waist under the bright mantle. It was embroidered with green silk, all designs worked by hand, and the edges were trimmed with gold thread. She gave it to Gawain and urged him to take it, unworthy as it was.

But he repeated that in no way could he accept either gold or gift before God has sent him the grace to achieve the purpose for which he had come.

"I beg you, do not be angry, but let the matter rest, for I can never agree to grant your request. I am indebted to you for your generosity, and will ever be your servant in fair or foul times." So gently did he try to put her off without displeasing her by his denial.

But the lady would not be gainsaid. "Do you reject this bit of silk because it is of so little value? Certainly it seems so." And she fondled and stroked the silk and it flowed through her fingers as she spoke. "Truly it seems a trifle and trifling is its worth. But if one only knew the qualities that are woven herein, he would value it more highly perhaps." She leaned close and put her red lips near his ear and spoke with soft sweet breath. "For any man who wears this green silk fastened firmly around his body, there is no man on earth can harm him, for he cannot be slain by any means."

Then Gawain pondered, weighing her words, and it came to his heart that this would be a talisman against the jeopardy that was waiting for him when he reached the chapel to find his fate. If he could escape unslain, the device were noble indeed! And he listened at last to her importunities and allowed her to speak. And she thrust the scarf upon him and bid him take it, and Gawain accepted it into his hands. She gave it to him with great delight and besought him, for her sake, never to reveal it and to keep it hidden from her lord. Gawain agreed that no man should ever know of it, but only they two. And he thanked her in great earnest, with heart and head. And the lady bent down and kissed the knight three times. Then she took her leave and left him there, for more pleasure from that man she could not obtain.

When she was gone, Gawain got up and attired himself in rich and noble array. He took up the love-token which the lady had given him and he hid it carefully away where he might find it later. Then he made his way to the chapel and he approached the priest privately and begged him to hear his confession and to instruct him how his soul might be saved when he should fare forth. And the priest shrove him surely and showed him his misdeeds, the lesser and the greater and sought mercy for him and gave absolution to the knight. He cleansed him of all sin in case his doomsday should fall on the morrow.

Then Gawain met with the ladies, and they were merry with song and carols and all kinds of pleasure, spending the day in happiness. He greeted each man courteously and they all agreed that never had they seen him so merry of mind since first he had come among them. Now let him linger in that lee, and love betide him!

The lord of the castle was still on the gallop, leading his men. He had fared far following the fox. As he leaped over a thicket to spy out the rascal, he heard the voice of the hounds that harried him closely, and saw Reynard running toward him through a rose grove, all the rabble in a rush right on his heels. The man waited quietly where he was until the creature drew near, then he drew forth his bright blade and threw it at the fox. The beast flinched from the spear and turned to retreat, but a hound dashed to him before he could move, and right there at the horse's feet they fell upon him and worried the wily fellow with wildest snarls.

The lord leaped down lightly and grabbed up the fox,

lifting it away from the hounds, and held it high over his head, and he "halloo"-ed loudly. The hounds barked and the hunters came with horns blowing high blasts, blowing the recall for the straying dogs. The noble company gathered and there was blowing of bugles, and those without shouted and cheered. It was the merriest company that men could hear of, that royal uproar raised for the sake of the fox. The handlers rewarded the hounds with strokes and fine words and fondled their heads in praise. Then they took up the fox and stripped off his coat.

They headed for home, for night was drawing nigh and they blew loud blasts on their mighty horns. The lord alighted at last at his home, found the fire upon the hearth and all the folk there beside it, and the good Gawain surrounded by the ladies. All greeted him with joy. Gawain wore a robe of blue velvet which fell to the ground and his surcoat was of soft wool and furred, and his hood lay upon his shoulders and was trimmed with ermine. And he greeted the lord in the middle of the floor, coming forward quickly from among the crowd. As he stepped forth, he said, "I shall fulfill our bargain first this time, that covenant we made when the wine flowed freely." And he embraced his host and kissed him three times with good spirit and right heartily.

"By heaven," responded the other, "You are gaining much good fortune in the winning of this wager, if these are your only profits."

"Yes, these are my gains," said Gawain, "and openly and completely paid, all that I have received today."

"Indeed, my gain is near worthless, for I hunted all day and naught have I had than this miserable fox—the devil take it!—and that is small return for those three kisses which you have brought me."

"Enough!" said Gawain, "We are quits, by the true cross." And the story of the fox was told as they stood there before the fire.

With mirth and minstrelsy, with as much meat as they wished, they made as merry as men might. Ladies and lords laughed at all the tables. Gawain and the good man were both happy, and if the company had become foolish with drink, so had they two, one more than the other. They made many a merry jape back and forth, man and company, until the time came that they must separate, each man to his bed, as night drew on. Then reluctantly the knight took his leave from his host and thanked him profusely for his hospitality.

"For such a happy sojourn as I have had here, and for your honor at this high festival, the good God bless you. I pledge you my fealty, to do your will; but I needs must, as you know, leave on the morrow. I ask that you will give me some fellow to show me, as you promised, the path to the Green Chapel, as God will require me to deal on the New Year's day the doom of my wyrd."

"Surely and with pleasure all that I have promised I shall render you," said the lord, and he assigned a man to set him upon his way and to conduct him through the countryside, so that he should have no trouble traveling through the firth and fields by the most direct route. Gawain thanked him for the great kindness that he showed him, and bowing to each, he took his leave of the two ladies. He spoke with them and kissed them and pressed his heartfelt thanks upon them, and they returned his words and commended him to heaven with many a sad sigh. And then from all that company he took courteous leave, thanking each man that he had met for his service and comfort and the special trouble which they had taken to serve him so well. Each man was as sorry to separate from him there as if they had been companions together for a lifetime.

Then he was led to his chamber and went to bed to get his rest. Whether he slept soundly I cannot say, for he had much on the morrow to trouble his thoughts. Let him be there at peace for now. Near enough is the fate he seeks, and soon enough I shall tell you how it worked itself out.

Chapter IX

O the New Year approached and the night passed, the dark driven away by the daylight, in God's good time. But wild weather walked the world. Clouds held the cold closely to the earth, with winds out of the north to torment the outcast. The snow fell in sharp blasts that cruelly slashed the shivering beasts. The shrieking winds blew down from the mountain and drove each dale full of drifts. The young man listened as he lay in his bed, for though he shut his eyes, little sleep did he get. With each cockcrow he was reminded of the appointed day.

He arose before daybreak in the light of the lamp that gleamed in his room. He called to his chamberlain, who answered immediately, and bid him bring his mail shirt and his saddle, and the man got up and fetched his raiment and prepared Gawain in proper fashion. First he dressed in clothes to keep out the cold, and then his harness was fastened on tightly, both the armor covering his stomach and his polished plate armor. And all was as good as new, thanks to the man who had wiped each piece until it shone. Gawain was happy to be on his way, and he gave orders to have his horse brought round to him.

Meanwhile he put on the most regal clothes: a red robe with seams embroidered with gold thread, furred within by fine skins, and with a badge of fine workmanship set as an ornament upon a patch of velvet, encrusted with gems set in gold. And he did not forget the lady's love-gift, no, Gawain did not forget to bring that to ensure his safety! After he had belted on his sword, he wrapped the green silk twice round his waist, and bright it gleamed against the red of his robe. But he did not wear it for its rich appearance or for pride in the polished pendants which gleamed on each end of the belt, but in order to save himself in this time of suffering, to help him bear the blow of the blade, the blow that he owed to the Green Knight. Then the young man hastened on his way, calling out thanks to all the assembled company.

Gringolet, huge and magnificent, was made ready, having been cared for in the castle stables, and eager to go was that proud horse. Gawain went to him and stroked his coat and spoke soberly to that gathering.

"Here in this castle is fine company indeed, and a good man who leads them—may he have joy! And that loveliest lady on earth—may good betide her! As they, out of charity, have entertained me as guest and showed me high honor by their hand, may God who rules on high bless them all! And if I may live on this earth for a while, I will perhaps be able to return your kindness."

Then he stepped into the stirrup and straddled his horse. His man handed him his shield and he took it upon his shoulder, tapped Gringolet with his golden heels and started across the courtyard pavement, Gringolet on the prance. His man, bearing spear and lance, mounted his horse and followed. Gawain shouted, "This castle and all within it I commend to God!" and he turned away. The bridge was let down and the broad gates unbarred and opened wide. Gawain again blessed all as he left and crossing the bridge he gave special thanks to the porter who knelt there.

He went on his way with the one servant who would show him how to get to that dismal place where he was to meet the rueful onslaught. They passed by banks where the bushes were bare; they climbed cliffs where the cold clung. The sky was clear above, but lowering clouds were heavy and threatening. A drizzling mist hung on the moors and melted on the mountains, where each hill had a hat of fog, a cloak of mist. Brooks bubbled and broke their banks, bright-shattering on the steep rocks as they splashed down in showers. Dreary and difficult was the path which they took, until at last it was time for the sun to rise. They were then on a high hill and snow covered all the countryside around them.

The servant who rode with him bade Gawain stop and rest. He looked at Gawain and spoke, "Well, I have brought you hither, man, at this appointed time, and you are not far from the place which I have spied out and inquired about. But I'll tell you the truth, and you know me as an honest man. I admire you, and if you'll take my advice you'll be the better for it.

"The place that you approach is held to be very perilous. There lives a creature in that wilderness who is the worst on earth. He is bold and grim, and he loves to strike blows. Fiercer is he than any man in middle-earth. His body is bigger than any four men of Arthur's court, bigger even than Hector. He makes sure that no man passes the Green Chapel, no matter how proud in valor, that he does not deliver him to death with a blow of his hand. For he is a metheless man and shows no mercy; and be it chaplain or churl who rides by the chapel, monk or mass-priest, or any other man, he thinks it as pleasant to quell one as another.

"Therefore I say, as I sit here in the saddle, if you proceed you will surely die although you had twenty lives to spend. Believe me, for I speak the truth. He has held this area in thrall for many years, determined to do battle in this field, and against his stout strokes you cannot defend yourself. So, I beg you, Gawain, let the man alone and get away while you can. Take some other direction, for God's sake. Ride for some other region as fast as you can, and I shall hie me home again. I promise you, I swear by God and all the saints and by the Holy Mother and everybody else, that I shall keep your secret and I shall never tell that I found you to flee from any man."

Gawain thanked the man somewhat grudgingly, and he spoke slowly, saying, "You mean well, good sir, and I know you wish me well. That you would keep my secret I believe; but though you kept it ever so closely, if I failed here and fled for fear of danger, as you suggest, then would I be a coward knight and I would never be excused.

"I will go to that Green Chapel, whatever may happen, and talk with that man as I must, work it weal or woe, as my wyrd demands. Even though he be a grim fellow to deal with, and his weapons fearful, yet does God have ways to protect His servants."

"Well," said the groom, "it is clear from what you say that you will bring ruin upon yourself, and if it pleases you to lose your life, I cannot stop you. Here—put your helmet on your head and take your spear in hand, and ride down this path past yon cliff, until you come to the bottom of that wild valley. Then look about off to the left a little and you shall see that chapel you seek right there in that valley, and the monstrous creature who keeps it.

"Now, fare-thee-well and may God keep you! For all the gold on earth I would not go with you, nor bear you fellowship through this wood one foot farther." And the groom gathered his reins and turned about to make his way back through the woods, urging his horse with his heels as hard as he might. Leaping across the fields, he went out of sight, leaving the man there by himself.

"With God's help," said Gawain, "I shall neither weep nor groan. I am bound to His will and I put myself in His hands."

Chapter X

E spurred Gringolet, and picking his path, he made his way along the side of the small copse and rode down the rough bank right into the dale. He rode slowly, and looked about, and he saw how wild it was, with no sign of refuge or shelter anywhere, but high, steep cliffs on both sides, rough, rugged crags with great, gnarled boulders. It seemed to him that the cliffs grazed the clouds. Then he halted and held up his horse a while, and looked everywhere seeking the chapel. He could not see it anywhere and he thought it strange.

Then he noticed across the field a mound, a barrow it was, a large, round-sided hillock near a bank at the water's edge, where a stream of water fell from the high rocks. The brook bubbled there as if it boiled. Gawain went over to the mound and, jumping down lightly, he fastened the reins to a linden tree, tying them to a rough branch. Then he turned toward the barrow and walked around it and around, wondering to himself what it might mean. It had a hole on each end and was overgrown with grass in uneven patches, and it was hollow within. Whether it was an old cave or perhaps the crevice of an old buried crag, he could not be sure.

"Oh, good Lord!" said Gawain. "Could this be the Green Chapel? Clearly the Devil must tell his matins at midnight here!"

Then he thought to himself, "Now surely this is a most desolate spot, ugly and overgrown with weeds, and a seemly place for that green man to deliver his devotions to the Devil. Now I suspect in my five wits that it is the fiend who has imposed this tryst upon me in order to kill me here. This is a chapel of mischance. Let destruction befall it! It is the most accursed place I have ever seen." And with his lofty helm on his head, his lance in his hand, he strode to the top of the mound.

Suddenly he heard a wondrously wild clamor from the high rocks beyond the brook, echoing back from the hills. It clattered against the cliffs as if to cleave them in two, and it was the sound of one sharpening a scythe against a grindstone. It whirred and grated like water through a mill. It made a rushing, ringing sound, frightful to hear.

"By God," said Gawain, "This is prepared in my honor, to greet me at journey's end!" Then he straightened and raised his head and looked to heaven. "Let God's will be done! To cry 'woe and alas' helps me not a bit. My life I here may give up, but dread shall not daunt me."

Then from the mound he called out loudly: "Who rules in this place to keep tryst with me? Now has the noble Gawain come! If any man has business with me, let him come here quickly, now or never, to make his needs known."

"Wait," said a voice from the cliffs high over his head, "and you shall have all that I once promised to you."

Yet the grinding noise continued for a while, the sound of an ax being turned on a whetstone, until suddenly the man appeared. He made his way out of a cleft, jumping from crag to crag and whirling a fearful weapon, a Danish ax, newly honed, with which to wield the blow, with a massive curved cutting edge at least four feet across. It was certainly no less than that in length, judging by the measure of the golden lacing that gleamed upon it. And the man was as green as he had been at their first meeting, from head to feet, locks and beard. He strode along, feet firm on the ground, using the ax like a staff, setting steel to stone and stalking beside it. When he came to the brook he did not wade across, but vaulted over with the help of the ax and came down on the near side.

Gawain went to meet the knight, but he did not make the customary bow of greeting. The Green Knight spoke first.

"Now, sir, our trysting time has come. God must guard you now. You are welcome, man, to my home, and you have timed your visit as a true man would. You remember the covenant struck between us: at this time twelvemonth ago you took what fell to your lot. Now I shall at this New Year requite you fully."

He looked around the snowy fields. Then he continued. "We are alone in this valley. There are no men to relieve us of this combat, falter or fall though we might. Take off your helm now and take your reward, and I pray you make no more debate about it than I did when you whipped off my head at a single wap!"

"No, by God," said Gawain, "I shall grudge you not at all for any hurt that may befall me. But limit yourself to one stroke only and I shall stand still and make no resistance to what you do." He leaned over and bowed his head and showed the white bare flesh as though he feared nothing. He did not dare to show fear.

Then the green man made himself ready. He lifted the grim ax with both hands, high over his head, to smite Gawain. All the strength in his body it took to hold it aloft. Gawain caught sight of that mighty ax as it came swishing down, and he flinched a little with his shoulders as if to draw away from the sharp blade. But the Green Knight, with a sudden jerk and swerve, checked the downward rush of the bright blade, and he let the ax fall onto the ground. For a moment he stared, and then he reproved the prince with burning words.

"You cannot be Gawain, he of great reputation, who has never shown fear in the face of any host of warriors, be it in hill or valley. Now you flinch for fear before you feel any hurt! I never heard such cowardice of Gawain. I neither flinched nor feared, man, when you were swinging the ax, nor did I make any objection at Arthur's court. My head tumbled to my feet and yet I did not flee. Now, before any harm is done, you tremble with the terror in your heart. Clearly I shall be called the better man!"

And Gawain said, "I shall not flinch again, sir! But when my head falls on the stones, I cannot restore it to its place. But briskly, man! Bring me to the point! Deal me my destiny and do it out of hand, for I shall stand you this stroke and shall start no more from the blow of the ax. Here, have my hand on it!"

"Have at you, then!" cried the other, and he heaved the bright blade aloft, and gathered his strength, standing stiffly as if made of wood. Again he feinted, bringing the blade down mightily, but he did not touch the man, withholding the ax suddenly before it could hit him. This time Gawain, as promised, awaited the blow and flinched with no member, but stood still as a stone or a stump that is embedded in rocky ground and held by a hundred roots.

Then mockingly the green man spoke: "So—now that I see you have a whole heart I will smite. Hold up the hood that Arthur gave you and bare your throat and let us see if it will survive this stroke."

Gawain spoke angrily. "Well, smite on! Man, you threaten too long! I think your heart shrinks within your own body."

"Forsooth, so boldly do you speak that I will not hesitate to satisfy you right now." And he took up his stance to strike and he tightened brow and mouth. Then he lifted the weapon. Gawain looked for no miracle, for now he had no hope of rescue.

The green man struck quickly, but he let down the blade gently with the edge just touching the bare neck. He did not hurt him, but nicked him lightly on the side of his neck, cutting the skin. The sharp blade penetrated to the flesh beneath the skin, so that the bright blood dripped to the ground. When Gawain saw the blood gleaming red on the snow, he leaped aside a spear-length, and he seized his helm and put it on his head. He twisted his shoulder to pull his shield forward from his back, and he pulled out his bright sword and he shouted aloud, for never since he was a little child born of his mother was he ever half so joyful as now.

"Cease now, monster! Offer me no more of your violence!

I have stood your stroke here without shrinking and if you inflict any more I shall readily repay you promptly and properly, be sure of that! Only one stroke is to befall me here, as our agreement promised, and therefore, good sir, hold!!"

Chapter XI

THE GREEN KNIGHT turned from him and leaned upon his ax, set the shaft to the ground and leaned upon the blade and looked at the lad who waited there. How steadfast, how fearless, and how bold he looked, how ready for battle! And he was pleased in his heart. He laughed with a ringing voice and spoke happily with the lad.

"Bold knight, upon this field of honor be not so fierce! No man here has used you dishonorably, nor treated you discourteously, but only as the decree at Arthur's court allowed. I owed you a stroke and you took it, so hold yourself well paid. I release you of any remnant of all other rights. If I had been more nimble, perhaps I could have wrought you a more harmful blow. First, I merely menaced you with a pretended blow and cut you with no cruel blade. That was for the agreement we made on that first night when you faithfully gave me the day's gains, as an honest man would. That second pretended blow was for the second day when you kissed my dear wife, which kisses you gave to me. And for both of those I offered you but two scant blows without scathe. For an honorable man is true to his word and he needs fear no danger.

"But on the third day you failed in that honor, and therefore you took that tap on the neck."

He looked at Gawain steadily, and Gawain at him, still as stone. And the green man continued.

"It is my garment you wear, that green silken girdle. My own wife offered it to you, I know. Ah, I know all about those kisses and your character also, and the wooing of my wife! I wrought all this myself. I sent her to test you. Truly I think that you must be the most faultless man that ever walked the earth. As a pearl in purity is to white peas, so is Gawain in virtue to all famous knights. But you fell short a little there, sir; you failed in faith. But it was not for intrigue, nor for lawless lust either, but because you loved your life, and I cannot blame you for that."

Gawain still stood like one stunned, so aggrieved with embarrassment that he cried for anguish inside. All the blood of his body burned in his face and he shrank for shame as the green man talked. He took off his helm and held it in his hands. At last he spoke wrathfully.

"Cursed be both cowardice and covetousness! In them is villainy and vice that destroys virtue!" And he caught up the pentangle and tore it loose and flung it roughly down. "Lo!— there is breaking of faith. Foul be its fall! I coveted my life and cowardice led me into fault for fear of your blow, made me forsake my nature, the generosity and loyalty that are a true knight's." And he bowed his head and wept bitterly. "Now am I false indeed and from fear have I fallen into treachery and deceit. Both bring only sorrow and shame. I confess to you, sir, here on this spot, that I have indeed been false to you in my conduct. If you will but allow me to regain your good will, I shall guard against its happening again."

Then the Green Knight laughed and said amiably: "I consider it entirely acquitted, any harm that I had. You have confessed freely and are aware of your failing and you have stood the sharp penance of my sword. I hold you cleansed of that fault and made as pure as if you had never transgressed since your birth. And I give you, sir, as a gift, that very scarf, as green as my own robe." He touched the silk at Gawain's waist lightly, and laid an arm across his shoulders.

"Sir Gawain, you may think upon this particular contest as you fare forth among the great and chivalrous knights of this world. Let this be the clear token of the adventure of the Green Chapel." Then he laughed and said merrily, "Now, you shall in this New Year come back again to my dwelling and we shall revel away the remainder of this festal time. With my wife, I promise, we shall certainly reconcile you, she who you thought was your keen enemy."

"No," said Gawain, and he took up his helm and looked sadly at the green man. "This has been a sorrowful journey. Good fortune betide you and may He who ordains all honor grant it to you! And commend me to that gracious lady, your comely companion, and the other lady, both the honored ladies who so cunningly beguiled this knight with their tricks.

"It is no great marvel to be made a fool of or to be won to sorrow through the wiles of a woman; for so was Adam, the first man on earth beguiled; and Solomon by many and various women; and Samson also, Delilah dealt him his wyrd! David was deluded by Bathsheba and suffered much woe. All these men were brought to disaster by woman's wiles.

"It would be a great gain to love them and yet to believe them not. But no man can do that. For these were the noblest men of old, all blessed above other men and yet they were all beguiled by women with whom they had dealings. To find myself in that company I think must be excused." Then he shook off sad thoughts.

"But your girdle I will accept with a right good will, not for the bright gold, nor for its magic—" here Gawain blushed again—"nor for the silk or fringed sides, nay, not for worth nor worship nor noble works. But as a symbol of my transgression I shall keep it always with me, a reminder, when I ride in renown, of the fault and frailty of feeble flesh, how susceptible it is to the stains of evil. And when pride of prowess inflates me, the sight of this will humble my heart.

"But one request I make, if it does not displease you: Since you are the lord of that land where I stayed with such pleasure, thanks to you, will you tell me your name? Only that and no more?"

"That I shall, certainly," replied the green man. "I am called Bercilak de Hautdesert in this land. Through the power of Morgan leFay, who lives in my house and has the skill of magical lore, all of this has happened. Morgan, the beautiful, the mistress of Merlin—many men has she taken, for she has had love dealings with that excellent wizard who knows all the knights of your court. Morgan the goddess is also her name. There is none so high in power or pride that she cannot tame!

"She sent me in that manner to your royal court in order to test the pride of its men, to see if the reputation of the Round Table were true. She sent me in that strange way to take away your wits and to frighten the fair Guenevere, to make her die with fear at the sight of that man who spoke with his head in his hand before that Table High. She took the form of that old one in my house, the ancient lady; she is in fact your aunt, the half-sister of Arthur, daughter of the Duchess of Tintagel, that lady upon whom the mighty Uther later fathered Arthur, who is your king.

"Therefore I entreat you, dear man, to come to your aunt and rejoice in my house. My court loves you, and I do as well, indeed, as any man under heaven."

But Gawain still refused. He would not under any conditions. So they embraced in friendship and saluted each other as fine princes and parted right there in the cold. Gawain, mounted on his fine horse, hastened homeward to Arthur's court and the Green Knight wended wheresoever he would.

Gawain rode then through many wild ways in the world on Gringolet. He had been given back his life, a fine gift indeed, and many a thought he gave to that strange event as he traveled. Sometimes he harbored in a house and sometimes out of doors. He had many adventures in the valley and he vanquished many, but I will not take time to tell all that in this tale.

The wound in his neck healed and he wore the green belt fastened like a baldric at his side, tied under his left arm, the end in a knot, as token of the fact that he was guilty of sin. And thus at last he came to the court, did Gawain the good knight.

Happiness sped through those halls when it was learned that Gawain had returned. Everyone thought it was a fine thing, indeed, and somewhat unlooked for. The king kissed the knight and the queen did also, and many knights sought him out to salute him and make inquiry of his wayfaring fortune. And he told the wondrous tale and confessed everything that had happened, the adventure at the chapel, the good will of the green man, the love of the lady, and the silk that he wore. He showed them the scar that he bore on his neck, the sign of his shameful disloyalty to the green man. He suffered when he told them and groaned with grief and mortification, and the blood burned in his face for shame when he spoke of it.

"Lo, lord," said Gawain to Arthur, as he held forth the silk, "here is the band of blame which I bear like the scar on my neck. This is the offense and the loss, the cowardice and covetousness that caught me there. This is the symbol of falsity in which I was taken. I will wear it all my life, for no one may hide his misdeed, nor may he undo it. Once guilt has touched a man, he is never free of it again."

And the king comforted the knight and all the court laughed and lovingly agreed on the spot that each man of the Table Round should henceforth wear such a baldric, the slanting ribbon of bright green, for the sake of that beloved man, and they would wear it with delight. And so it came to be accorded as the renown of the court and always afterwards anyone who wore it was especially honored.

So in Arthur's day this adventure occurred, as books of romance will witness. Many strange and curious wonders have happened in Britain since the days of Brutus whose race came from Troy. But surely this tale of Gawain and his contest with the Green Knight in a trial of honor and faith is one of the most wondrous.

GLOSSARY

All Saints' Day November 1, a general celebration of saints, instituted in the 7th century.

Baldric A belt or girdle worn pendent from one shoulder across the breast and under the opposite arm, used to support a shield, sword, or bugle.

Barbican Outer fortification or defense of a castle, especially a double tower erected over a gate or bridge; serves as a watchtower.

Bare-mote A single note of the hunting horn or bugle; the three-bare-mote is a series of three single notes.

Brache A kind of hound which hunts by scent.

Cozen To play the crafty knave; to cheat or defraud; more usually, to beguile, to while away time.

Cuisse Body armor to protect the front part of the thighs.

To dree the wyrd (or weird) To endure one's fate; to suffer or submit to one's destiny.

French Flood The English Channel.

Gauntlet A glove made of leather covered with flexible plates of steel.

Halberd A combination spear and battle ax, consisting of a sharp-edged blade ending in a point, and a spear head, mounted on a handle five to seven feet long.

Hauberk Defensive armor intended for protection of neck and shoulders; also later (12th–13th centuries) a military tunic of ring or chain mail flexible to motions of the body.

Helm Metal helmet, often crested, sometimes displaying sign of rank or other identification.

Kennet A small hunting dog.

Matins   A canonical office, or prayer, recited at daybreak.

Metheless   Immoderate, intemperate, merciless.

Michaelmas   29 September, the feast of Saint Michael.

Poleyn (polayn)   A piece of defensive body armor covering the knee.

Sabaton   A broad-toed metal foot-covering, a piece of defensive body armor protecting the top of the foot from ankle to toes.

Spinney   A thorn-hedge; a brambled wood or copse; a thicket.

Trochet   Ornamental spire, similar to the tines of a deer's antlers, used in decorating and embellishing the towers or turrets of a castle.